DAVID SHANNON

TOO MANY TOYS

THE BLUE SKY PRESS

An Imprint of Scholastic Inc. • New York

To my excellent neighbors,
the Carr family

THE BLUE SKY PRESS

Copyright © 2008 by David Shannon
All rights reserved.

For information regarding permission, please
write to: Permissions Department, Scholastic Inc.,
557 Broadway, New York, New York 10012.

SCHOLASTIC, THE BLUE SKY PRESS, and
associated logos are trademarks and/or
registered trademarks of Scholastic Inc.

LEGO is a trademark of Kirkbi Ag.
Used without authorization.

Library of Congress catalog card number: 2007044753
ISBN-10: 0-439-49029-4 / ISBN-13: 978-0-439-49029-0
20 19 18 17 16 15 14 13 12   18 19 20
Printed in Malaysia   108
First printing, October 2008

SPENCER HAD TOO MANY TOYS.
They covered the floor of his bedroom and piled up in his closet. They were stashed under his bed. They spilled down the stairs and into the living room.

He had big toys in the backyard . . .

and little toys in the bathtub.

Sometimes Spencer played with nice, quiet wooden pull-toys. Other times he played with noisy, crazy electronic toys. He had puzzles, board games, and talking books that fueled his mind . . .

and loud, jumpy, frenzied
video games that fried it.

Spencer liked to make his toys into a
parade that stretched from one corner
of the house to the other and back again!
There was an entire zoo of stuffed animals
and a gigantic army of little action figures.

He had a fleet of planes, trains, and toy boats, and a convoy of miniature trucks and cars.

He also had lots and lots of
musical instruments, art supplies,
and alien spaceman weapons.

Everyone gave toys to Spencer. Of course, his mom and dad did. But so did Grandma Bobo and Poppy and Grandiddy and Auntie Mim and Uncle Fred and Cousin Drew. They gave him toys for every holiday (even the 4th of July!) and his birthday.

He also got toys from all his friends on his birthday, and on their birthdays, too, when he went to their parties!

He got toys at the Drive-thru with his Kidburger, and at school for having lots of Peace Person Points, and at the dentist and the doctor when he didn't squirm.

THAT'S A LOT OF . . .

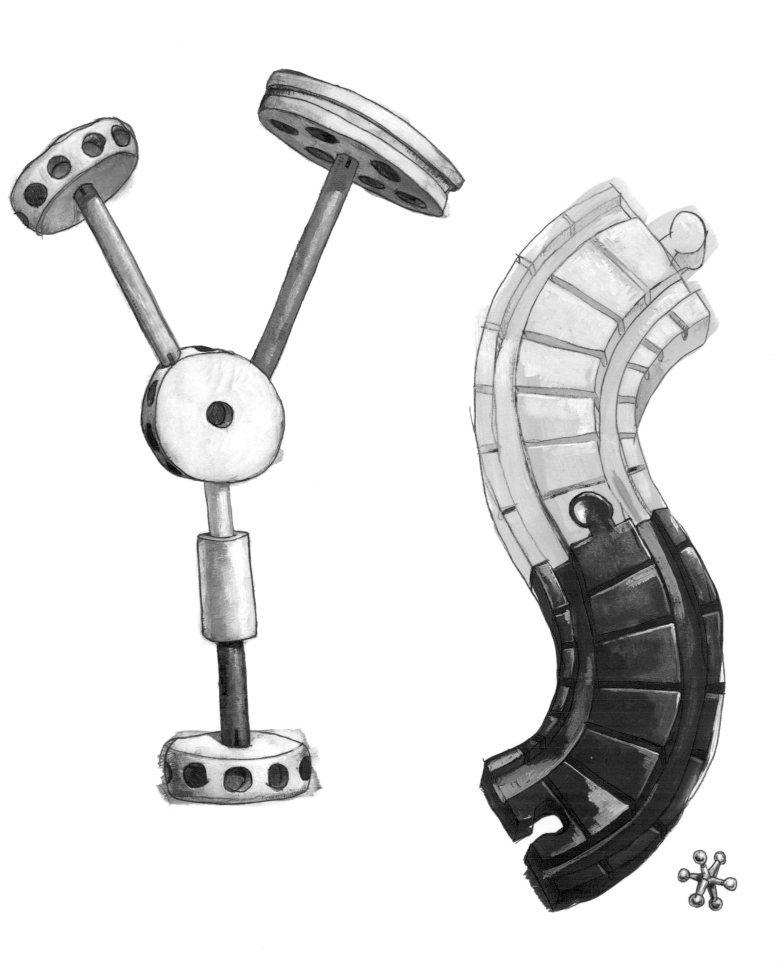

They were becoming a household hazard.
Have you ever stepped on a Lego piece in
your bare feet? Or a jack? Well, it really hurts!
Especially if you weigh as much as Spencer's dad.

You can also trip on things
like railroad tracks and race
cars if you're carrying
a load of laundry.

One day, Spencer's mom had had it up to here with
all the toys. "SPENCER!" she yelled on her way upstairs.
"YOU HAVE TOO MANY TOYS!"

That's impossible! thought Spencer.

Then she said, "We're going to get rid of some of them."

That's a CATASTROPHE!

"Pick out which toys you don't want," she ordered,
"and put them in this box."

"BUT I LOVE THEM ALL!" Spencer cried.

"All right," his mother said. "I'll help you." She picked up an Alien Space Ninja. "How about this one? You haven't played with this in years."

"But I was just about to!"

"Spencer," his mother said, "it doesn't have a head."

"I'm making him a new one!" Spencer replied.

"Fine," said Spencer's mother. "But this can definitely go." She put down the Alien and picked up a filthy, one-eared bunny.

"Not Mr. Fluffers! Mom, how could you!"

"This one then," she said.

"That's Mr. Fluffers' best friend!"

"This one?"

"Mother, have you forgotten? Grandma Bobo gave me that on my fourth birthday. And I'll never be four again—EVER!"

"Oh, please, Spencer," said his mom, rolling her eyes. "Don't be so dramatic!"

"Okay," she said, "you can keep that one. But I'm giving away this pig and the Johnny Choo-choo."

"Tell you what," countered Spencer. "I'll let you have the pig, but I get Johnny Choo-choo."

"What are you, a lawyer now?!" asked Spencer's mother. "You can keep Johnny Choo-choo, but the cow goes in the box, too. Deal?"

"How about two Gitchigoomies instead," said Spencer,
"and I'll throw in a Little Peeper of your choice."

"How about all of them go in the box, or you don't watch
TV for a week."

Spencer decided it was in his best interest to agree. "Deal!"

"Finally, some toys in the box," sighed Spencer's mom. "I
had no idea this would be so much work!"

She plopped down on the floor next to an egg-shaped pirate that bellowed, "ARR, AVAST YE SCURVY DOG! AVAS . . . ARSCURVY YOG! DURVY OG . . . DURVY OG!"

"Here's another one you can do without," she said.

"No problem," said Spencer.

His mom nearly fell over. "What!?! You're going to give it up, just like that?"

"Sure," Spencer replied. "That's Dad's."

So Spencer and his mom went through every
toy box and looked in every closet and under
every bed until they had haggled and wrestled
and argued over every toy in the entire house.
Finally, they were finished, and his mom had
a cup of hot tea and a short rest.

Then she went upstairs to begin loading the toys into the car. But instead of a nice, neat box of toys all ready to go, she saw a big, messy pile of toys all over the floor!

"SPENCER!" she screamed. "WHAT HAVE YOU DONE?! WE HAD A DEAL!!"

"You were right, Mom!" Spencer called from his bedroom. "I do have too many toys. But we can't give away this box…

KEEP OUT!

PARKING FOR SPENCER ONLY

"It's the best toy EVER!"